Nayan's Family Fruit Salad

Navjit Sandhu

Illustrations by Anthony Erazo Santos

◆ FriesenPress

Suite 300 - 990 Fort St
Victoria, BC, V8V 3K2
Canada

www.friesenpress.com

9215 120 St
North Delta, BC, V4C 6R8
Canada

navisandhu00@gmail.com
www.navjitsandhu.com

ISBN
978-1-5255-2975-7 (Hardcover)
978-1-5255-2976-4 (Paperback)
978-1-5255-2977-1 (eBook)

1. JUVENILE FICTION, COOKING & FOOD

Distributed to the trade by The Ingram Book Company

This book belongs to me.

My name is:

_____

Thank you!

This book is with endless love for my children Nirvaan and Sahaas. It is also for all of the other wondrous children who have inspired this book. Nirvaan and Sahaas, thank you for choosing me as your mom. Thank you for being my greatest teachers, and helping me to continue to grow and evolve.

READ

A Note To:

Parent, grandparents, aunts, uncles, friends, educators, and other loved ones

Children learn to love books and reading when we share our enthusiasm, and love of reading with them.

READ ALOUD:
To stimulate language development, curiosity, memory, and listening skills.

ECOURAGE CHILDREN TO ACTIVELY ENGAGE & PARTICIPATE :
Allowing them to expand their imagination, and share their ideas, thoughts, and feelings.

ASK OPEN ENDED QUESTIONS AS YOU READ:
To encourage problem solving and cognitive (intellectual) skills.

DEVELOP AND PROMOTE INTIMACY:
Reading to children helps them bond with you, and feel close to you. The feeling of being loved lifts them up, and strengthens their positive self-esteem, and boosts their confidence. At the same time, it gives them a sense of security, enhancing and strengthening their relationship with you.

Hi! My name is Nayan Singh,

and this is my pet lion,

Sher Singh.

Sat Sri Akaal!

Today we are going to have a picnic at the park with my grandparents Dada Ji and Dadi Ji, and my little Veer Ji, Shaan Singh.

At my house, my grandparents don't understand English very well,

and Punjabi.

My family loves to eat healthy fruit salad.
Sher Singh and I are going to pack a basket
so that we can have a snack at the park.

Would you like
to help us?

1 ikk keeri

My little **Veer Ji**, Shaan Singh, that's my baby brother,

really likes to eat bananas.

Should we pack a yummy yellow banana for **Veer Ji**?

In Punjabi we call a banana **kela**.

Can you say banana in Punjabi?

Kela. That's right. Good job. Let's all say it together. **Kela**!

Let's find the **kela**, and put it in the basket.

(Sing to the tune of "Where is Thumbkin" or "Frere Jacques")

Find the **kela**, find the **kela**

There it is, there it is

Put it in the basket, put it in the basket

Right here, right here.

2 doh keerian

Shukryia, thank you for helping us

put the **kela** in the basket.

Dada Ji, that's my grandpa, enjoys eating grapes.

Should we pack some juicy green grapes for Dada Ji?

In Punjabi we call grapes **angoor**.

Let's all say it together... **Angoor!**

Wonderful, that's exactly how you say it.

Let's find some **angoor** and pack them into our basket.

(Sing to the tune of "Where is Thumbkin" or "Frere Jacques")

Find the **angoor**, find the **angoor**

There they are, there they are

Put them in the basket, put them in the basket

Right here, right here.

You are so smart!

Shukryia, thank you for helping us pack the angoor into the basket.

3 tinn keerian

Dadi Ji, that's my grandma, just loves to eat sweet mangoes.

Do you think we should pack some marvelous mangoes for Dadi Ji?

We call mangoes **aambh** in Punjabi.

Can you say **aambh**?....Aambh!

Brilliant! Now let's all say it again together. **Aambh**!

Now, let's find the **aambh**, so that we can pack it into our basket.

(Sing to the tune of "Where is Thumbkin" or "Frere Jacques")

Find the **aambh**, find the **aambh**

There it is, there it is

Put it in the basket, put it in the basket

Right here, right here.

Wow, you did a super job of finding the **aambh**. **Shukriya**! Thanks!

4 chaaR keeRian

Oh dear, we forgot to pack my favourite fruit. I love all types of fruit. My most favourite is the orange.

Do you think we should pack a nice sweet orange for me?

We call an orange **santra** in Punjabi.

Can you say **santra**?... **Santra**!

Fantastic! Now let's all say it again together, really loud. **Santra**!

Let's find the **santra** and put it in the basket.

(Sing to the tune of "Where is Thumbkin" or "Frere Jacques")

Find the **santra**, find the **santra**
There it is, there it is
Put it in the basket, put it in the basket
Right here, right here.

Wow, you did a super job of finding the **santra**. Let's put it in the basket. **Shukriya**, thanks!

5 panj keerian

I think we have a fruit for everyone. We have Veer Ji's Kela, Dada Ji's angoor, Dadi Ji's aambh and my santra. Does everyone have a fruit?

Oops. We forgot someone. Who did we forget?

Oh, that's right we forgot about Sher Singh.

Sher Singh likes to eat crunchy red apples.

Do you think we should pack some apples for him?

We call apples saeb in Punjabi.

Can you say saeb?.... Saeb!

Delightful! Let's all say it again together. Saeb!

Let's find the saeb and put them in the basket.

(Sing to the tune of "Where is Thumbkin" or "Frere Jacques")

Find the saeb, find the saeb

There they are, there they are

Put them in the basket, put them in the basket

Right here, right here.

WOW, you did an excellent job of finding the saeb and putting them in the basket.

Shukriya!

Thank you very much for helping us today.

Sher Singh and I could have never packed this basket without all of your help. Now we can meet the rest of our family at the park for an afternoon full of fun and healthy fruit salad.

Translation of Words

 Sat Sri Akaal: Greeting for hello/good bye

 Dada Ji: Grandfather (father's father, also known as Baba Ji)

 Dadi Ji: Grandmother (father's mother)

 Veer Ji: Brother (can refer to cousin brother as Veer Ji as well)

 Kela (khay-la): Banana

 Angoor (ung-goor): Grape(s)

 Aambh (aam-bh): Mango

 Santra (sun-traa): Orange

 Saeb (sabe): Apple

 Shukriya (shuk-ree-a): Thank you

Translation of Words Continued...

Keeri (kee-ri): Ant

Keerian (kee-ri-an): Ants (plural)

1 ikk keeri: One ant

2 doh keerian: Two ants

3 tinn keerian: Three ants

4 chaar keerian: Four ants

5 panj keerian: Five ants

CPSIA information can be obtained
at www.ICGtesting.com
Printed in the USA
BVHW020833010320
573631BV00015B/56

9781525529757